FANTASTIC CREATURES & CRYPTOZOIDS

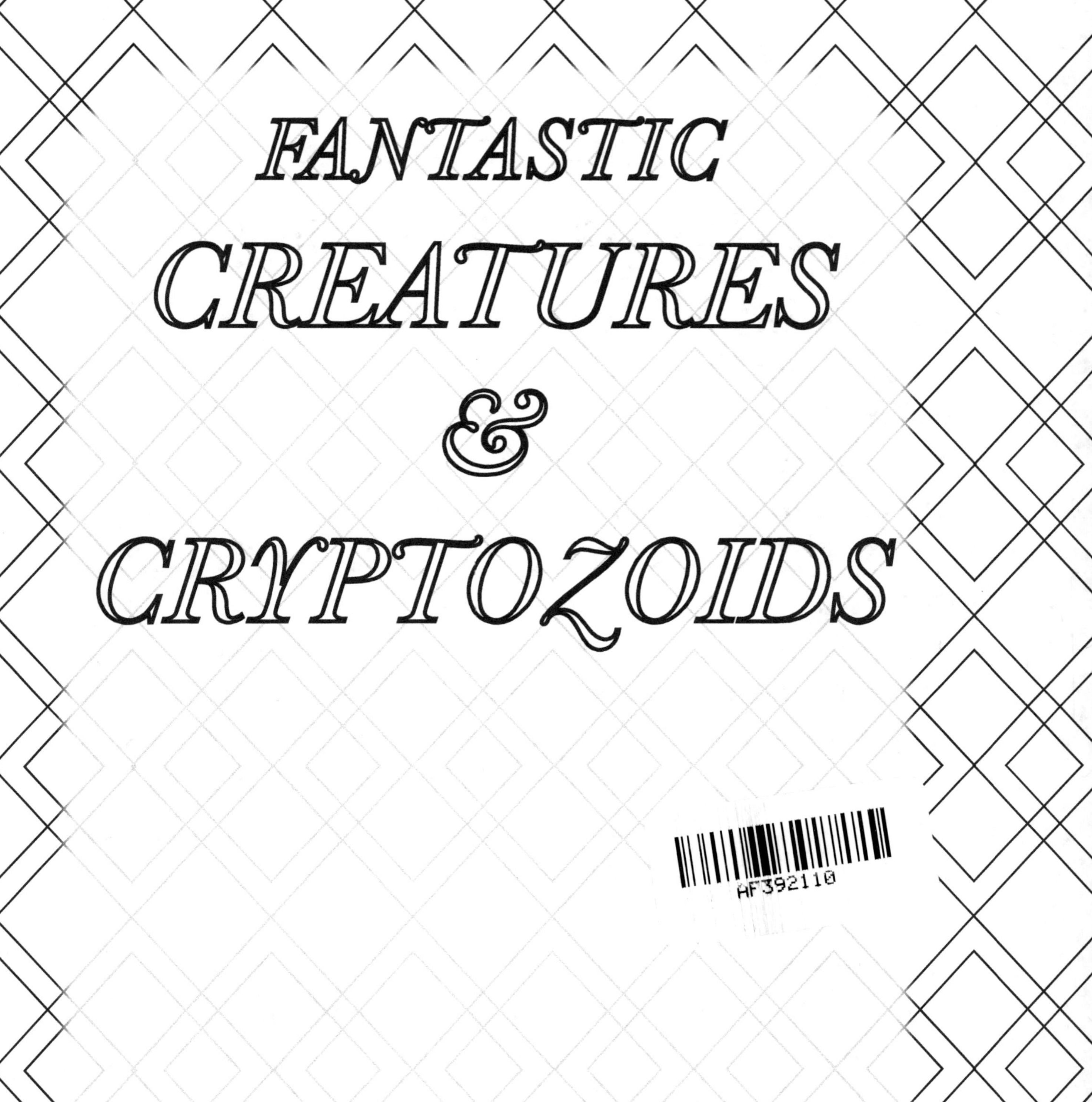

written & illustrated by james k. wadley

SIX-EYED SALAZANDER

description
species Reptilian
color Dark earth-tones
average weight 180–230 kgs.
average length (*body*) 2.5–4 meters (*tail*) 2–3 meters

abilities
The salazander's skin is very durable and can change different shades of color to adapt to most environments. Its prehensile tail can be used as a sharp whip or as a fifth arm, to grab or hold something or to pull itself up. The salazander's head is an exo-skull that protects its fangs and digestive tongues.

characteristics
The Six-Eyed Salazander is an evolved hunter species. Although they prefer warmer, jungle climates, they are equally adept at hunting their prey in deep waters or sandy deserts. Salazanders usually travel in pairs or in packs of three, but individually they prefer isolation and rarely develop families.

GRAND PHOENIX

description
species Avian
color Bright fire tones
average weight 20–30 kgs.
average length (*body*) 2.5–3 meters (*tail*) 2–3 meters (*wingspan*) 2–3x the body length

abilities
The Phoenix is an immortal bird that is reincarnated constantly through a process of fiery death and rebirth. The Phoenix is extremely strong and has a magical voice that is mystical and soothing to hear. It also has the ability to change its form into a human body.

characteristics
Associated with the sun, the Phoenix both controls and is, in turn, controlled by fire. As a force of nature, there is only one Phoenix at any given time, growing increasingly powerful as it repeats the continuous cycle of life. Throughout many different cultures, it is most often a symbol for hope, strength, and longevity.

ABOMINABLE YETI

description
species Bestial carnivore
color Polar white
average weight 600–700 kgs.
average height (*upright*) 4–7 meters

abilities
The Yeti is a large, ape-like, bipedal creature that is incredibly strong. It is covered in a thick white fur that insulates it from cold weather. It is often depicted with sharp claws, fangs, and/or horns that are necessary for hunting and defending itself.

characteristics
Also known as the "Abominable Snowman", the Himalayan Yeti is often connected to the North American "Bigfoot" because of their similar appearance and mannerisms. Due to the lack of actual evidence to suppport their existence, however, Yetis and other "Missing Link" creatures are a controversial subject of scientific debate.

LYCANTHROPE

description
species Bestial carnivore
color Host dependent (see *characteristics*)
average weight 3x the host's weight
average height 1.5x the host's height

abilities
A lycanthrope, or "werewolf", is a normal human with the ability to transform into a larger feral state, with heightened senses and strength, elongated claws and fangs, and a propensity for hunting.

characteristics
Lycanthropes are usually the victims of a curse or dark magic, and the transformation process, which only takes place under a full moon, is extremely painful. In "werewolf" form, they are driven by blood-thirsty hunger and animalistic rage, but are then filled with guilt and despair when they revert back to normal human form.

PEGASUS

description
species Equine
color Variable (dark brown to bright white)
average weight 800–900 kgs.
average height (*body*) 20–22.5 hh (*tail*) 4–4.5 meters
(*wingspan*) 15–20 meters

abilities
Pegasus can run faster than any animal on land and fly higher than any creature in the air. Along with the power to transport themself and a rider to other magic realms, Pegasus could also create wondrous springs of water that inspired early artists and poets.

characteristics
Pegasus is a winged horse created by the divine will of the Greek God Poseidon and was the transportation of choice to generations of heroes and deities. Accordingly, Zeus later transformed Pegasus into a constellation of stars which continues to inspire modern astrologers as well as astrophysic scientists.

MERMAID

description
species Aquatic mammal
color Greenish-blues
average weight 140–190 kgs.
average height (*body*) 1.5–2 meters (*tail*) 2–3 meters

abilities
Mermaids are half female and half fish or sea serpent and can breathe and function underwater as well as on dry land (different types of mermaids can transform their tails into legs). Traditionally they have enchanting, hypnotic voices which they sometimes use to lure sailors into storms and hidden dangers.

characteristics
While some Mermaids can be destructive, others have been know to grant magical wishes to or fall in love with a human. Comparable to the Greek Sirens and other cultural sea nymphs, Mermaids are usually described as either incredibly beautiful or a monstrous sea-witch.

UNICORN

description
species Equine
color Rainbows
average weight 750–800 kgs.
average length (*body*) 18–20 hh (*tail*) 5–8 meters

abilities
A Unicorn's powers emanate from its unique single fore-head horn, which can cure poisons and other sicknesses. They have been known to grant wishes or to bring good fortune to humans.

characteristics
Unicorns are peaceful but wild, and can only be tamed by a virgin. Its horn is comprised of a substance known as *alicorn*, which was alleged to have both magical and medicinal properties. Originally associated with purity and grace, Unicorns have also come to symbolize fantasy as well as extremely rare commodities.

HARPY

description
species Avian
color Green skin, rainbow-colored wings
average weight .5–190 kgs.
average height (*body*) .5–1 meter (*wingspan*) .5–1 meter

abilities
Harpies are wind spirts that can fly very fast and use their talons to snatch up their prey. Because they emit pheremones, Harpies can mentally control people or put them to sleep by touch.

characteristics
Harpies are usually described as ugly and cruel. They have a violent hatred of humans and often prefer to play vicious tricks and torture their victims instead of killing them. Harpies have an insatiable appetite for revenge and punishment.

GRIFFIN

description
species Hybrid
color Tan/brown fur, grey/white feathering
average weight 600–1000 kgs.
average height (*body*) 3–5 meters (*wingspan*) 2–4 meters

abilities
Griffins have the strength of a lion and the flying ability of an eagle. As a creature of magic, feathers from its wings were used to cure blindness and consuming a Griffin's blood was thought to prolong life.

characteristics
Griffins have a deep love of gold and has a tendency to make nests surrounded by gold nuggets. Griffins are noble and very protective, especially of their family, and choose only one mating partner for life.

BASILISK

description
species Reptilian
color Green, orange, yellow
average weight 75–990 kgs.
average length (*body*) 4–8 meters (*tail*) 3–5 meters

abilities
The Basilisk is dangerously venomous, and its saliva and bodily secretions are pure poison. It can see through darkness and fatally hypnotize its prey. The Basilisk does have a peculiar weakness: the odor of weasels.

characteristics
Because of their great size, the Basilisk is known as the King of Serpents. They are usually bred by dark wizards for nefarious reasons, such as terrorizing villagers or poisoning royalty. It is considered to be a creature made up of pure evil.

IRON GOLEM

description
species Anthropomorphic elemental
color Browns or greys
average weight 200–300 kgs.
average height 3–8 meters

abilities
Golems are made of inanimate material and cannot be killed or destroyed by conventional means. Although some unique Golems have shown unique magical powers such as invisibility, most Golems are simply large and extremely strong.

characteristics
A Golem is a handmade, often sculpted by clay, monster that is a servant to Jewish rabbis or magicians. While they are created to obey their master's whims, Golems have been known to violently break free from enslavement and cause their own chaos and destruction.

FLYING SNAKE (WHISPERING DEATH)

description
species Reptile
color Red, green, black
average weight 40–90 kgs.
average length 1–6 meters

abilities
The Whispering Death is a small, carnivorous dragon that can fly as well as burrow into the ground. It has six rows of fangs and many layers of poisonous spikes along its hide that can be used as projectile weapons.

characteristics
The Whispering Death is a vicious predator that can suddenly appear from its underground burrows and attack with vicious precision. Although they hate sunlight, when they fly they will do so in defensive spiral patterns. They have instinctively long memories and never let go of a grudge.

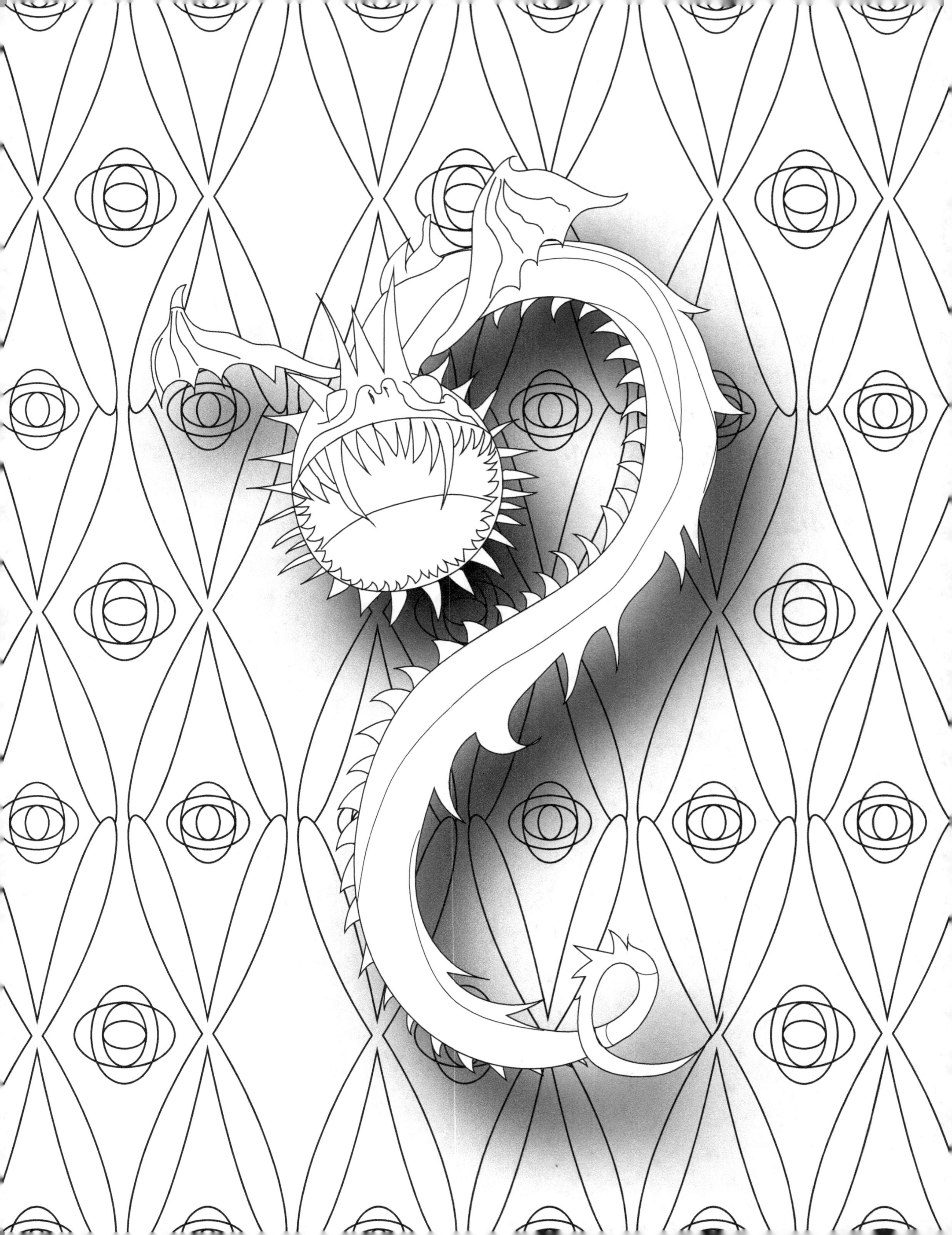

MOTHMAN

description
species Hybrid
color Dark tones with red eyes
average weight 150–250 kgs.
average height (*body*) 2–3 meters (*wingspan*) 3–5 meters

abilities
The Mothman is a human-sized bird that can fly and
has heightened strength. Although people experience a
deep and profound fear upon sight, the Mothman is not
actually violent or evil.

characteristics
The Mothman is an urban legend whose presence has
been alleged at a number of human disaster events
going all the way back to early 17th century Native
American folklore. Whether it has an alien origin or is
some type of mutated creature, the Mothman doesn't
seem to be able to control its own prophetic powers.

CHUPACABRA

description
species Reptilian canine
color Variable (see ***characteristics***)
average weight 200–500 kgs.
average length 1-6 meters

abilities
Chupacabras are vampiric and drink blood to survive. They are stealthy hunters, and leave recognizable bite-marks on their victims due to their unusual teeth. They also have defensive spikes or quills on their back.

characteristics
Chupacabras have a variety of reported descriptions, from a sick, mangy dog to a demonic lizard. Although frightening in appearance, Chupacabras usually shy away from people and prefer to feast on livestock, such as goats and cows. It exists in Puerto Rico and other parts of Latin America.

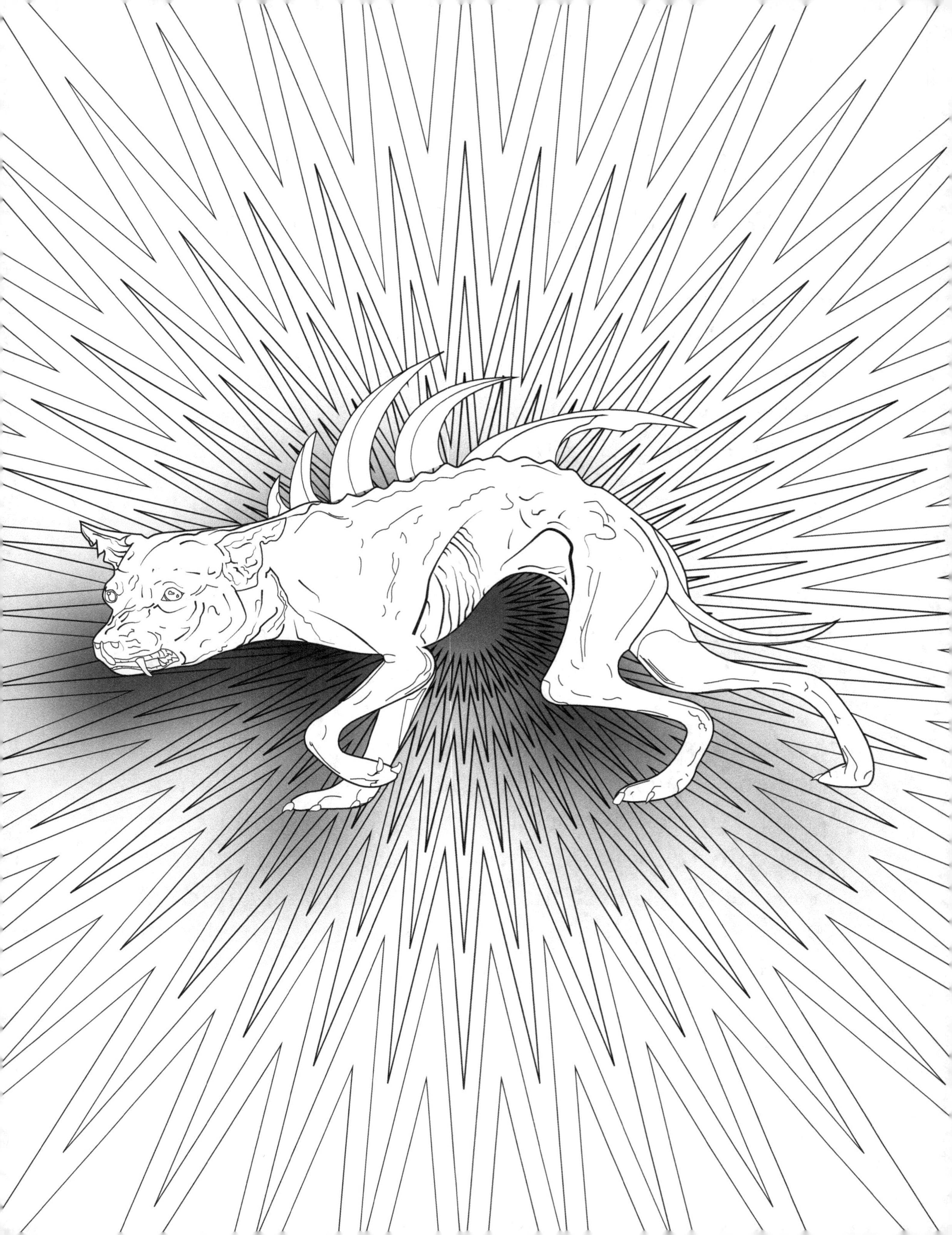

LOCH NESS CREATURE ("NESSIE")

description
species Plesiosaur
color Lime-green with bluish highlights
average weight 4000–15000 kgs.
average length 25–30 meters

abilities
"Nessie" is the world's most famous living dinosaur. It is
a water-based creature that is benevolent in nature.
Other than its enourmous size, the Loch Ness Creature
has few, if any, offensive capabilities.

characteristics
Located in the Scottish Highlands, sightings of the Loch
Ness Creature have been a controversial source of proof
for cryptozoologists. Most of the evidence of the Loch
Ness Creature's existence is based on either informal
witnesses or simply fake, as there is a large market for
"Nessie" branded merchandise.

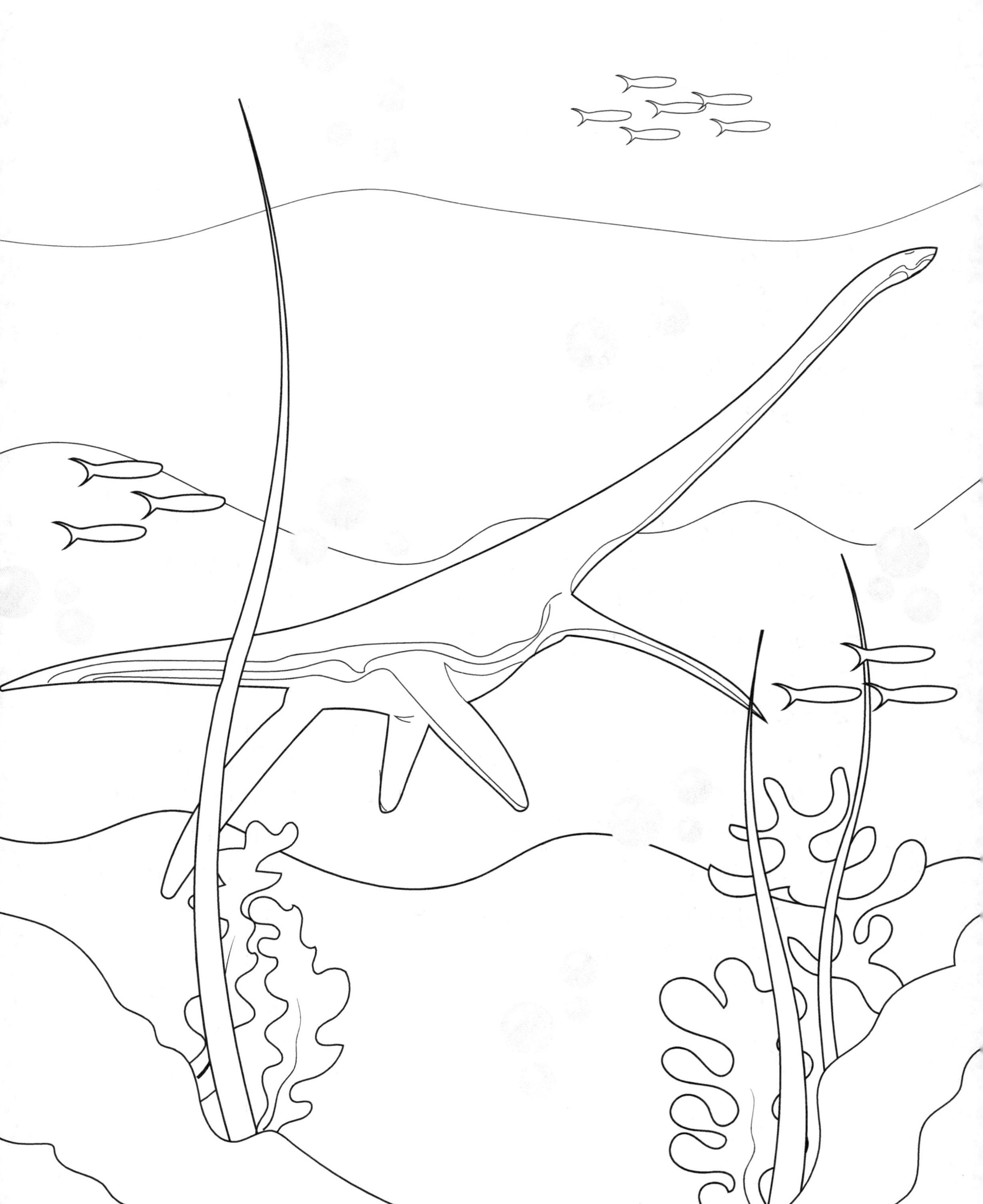

WENDIGO

description
species Bestial carnivore
color Polar white
average weight 700–800 kgs.
average height 4–7 meters

abilities
The Wendigo has the strength and ferocity of a large bear or ape. It has cannibal tendencies, craving the taste of human flesh. Its appearance is often preceded by a sudden cold and freezing wind.

characteristics
The Wendigo is an evil spirit that possesses a person and alters their form into blood-thirsty mosters, similar to Lycanthropes. Mostly based in and around the forests of Canada, the "Wendigo psychosis", or the urge to eat people, spread from the First Nation communities to early European explorers.

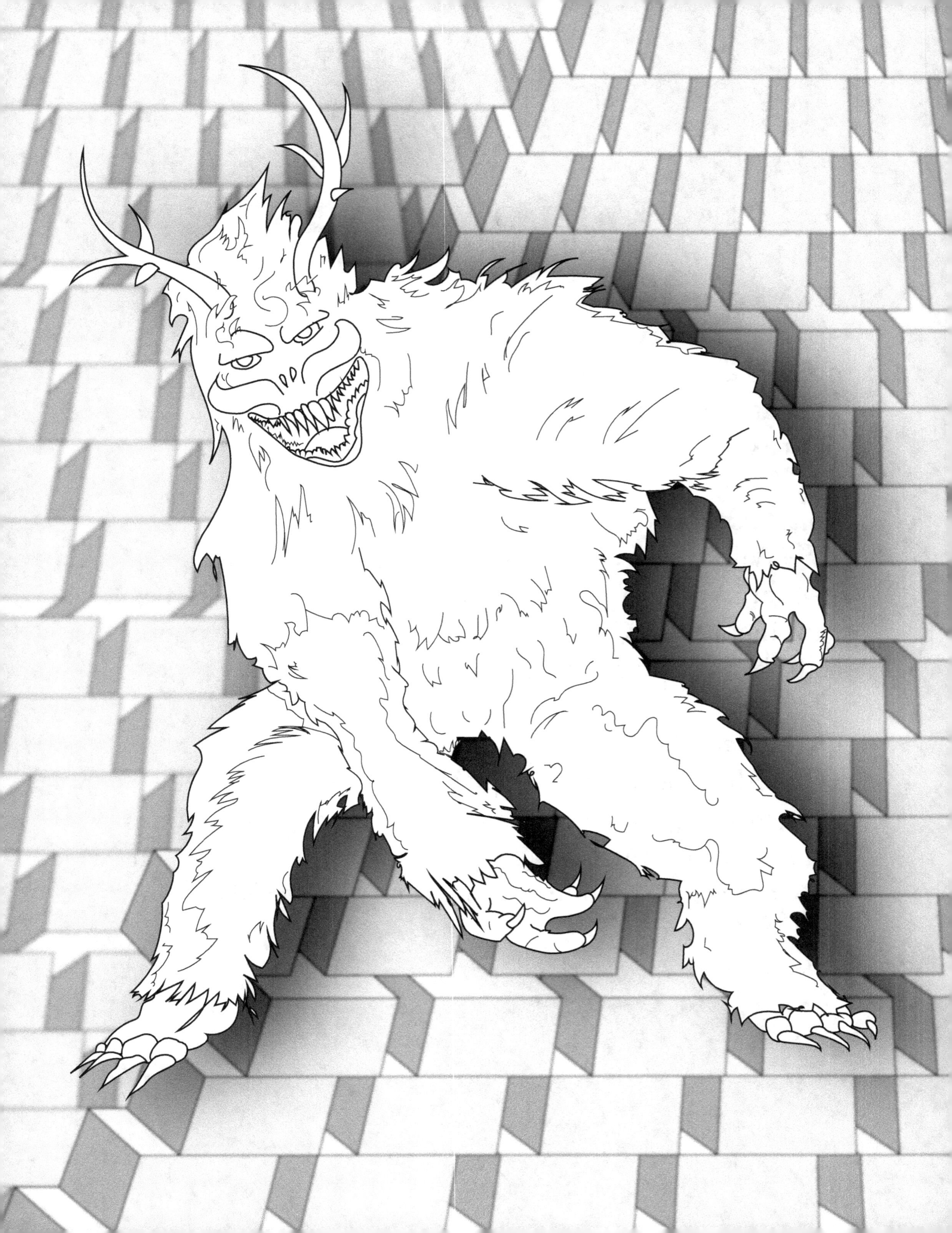

WILL O'THE WISP

description
species Energy source
color Variegated spectrum
average weight Not applicable
average height Not applicable

abilities
The Will o'the Wisp is a ghostly light that appears as energy or flame that is bright but not hot. It has a calming and spiritual effect, often appearing to people right before their deaths.

characteristics
Will o'the Wisps are lost spirits that are usually seen over swamps, bogs, and marshes. They are sometimes attributed to organic gasses from decaying plants, but they are also associated with wish-granting fairies.

<u>JERSEY DEVIL</u>

description
species Forest creature
color Black and brown wings and fur, fiery red highlights
average weight 20–140 kgs.
average height (*body*) 1–3 meters (*wingspan*) 2–4 meters

abilities
The Jersey Devil has many attributes and abilities of various different animals, such as wings for flight, a snake's tail, and bestial fangs and claws. It has even been known to hop like a kangaroo.

characteristics
As the name implies, the Jersey Devil inhabits the Pine Barrens of New Jersey. Often described as emitting a "high-pitched blood-curdling scream". According to local legend, the Jersey Devil was the demonic child of a witch named Mother Leeds.

Cryptozoids checklist

- ☐ 01. Six-eyed Salazander
- ☐ 02. Grand Phoenix
- ☐ 03. Abominable Yeti
- ☐ 04. Lycanthrope
- ☐ 05. Pegasus
- ☐ 06. Mermaid
- ☐ 07. Unicorn
- ☐ 08. Harpy
- ☐ 09. Griffin
- ☐ 10. Basilisk
- ☐ 11. Hydra v. Kraken v. Chimera
- ☐ 12. Iron Golem
- ☐ 13. Flying Snake (Whispering Death)
- ☐ 14. Mothman
- ☐ 15. Chupacabra
- ☐ 16. Loch Ness Creature ("Nellie")
- ☐ 17. Wendigo
- ☐ 18. Will o' the Wisp
- ☐ 19. Jersey Devil